for no one in particular,
though a few people did come to mind while writing this book

A CAGE for the WIND

a story of gradually-realized insanity
told in poetry and prose

by DAVE MATTHES

This book is a work of fiction.
None of it is to be taken in a literal sense or meant with offensive intentions unless otherwise specifically mentioned. Any resemblances to actual events that occur in exactly the same fashion involving any persons, locales, or incidents is entirely coincidental. Any names of actual persons that have been used within the contents of the story are used in a purely fictional state to drive the motion of the story and its characters.

Independently published and printed in the United States by AMAZON.

Front and back cover design by Dave Matthes.

ISBN: 9798713425593

Also by Dave Matthes
available on Amazon

NOVELS
The Slut Always Rides Shotgun
The Passive Aggressors
In This House, We Lived, and We Died
Sleepeth Not, the Bastard
Bar Nights
Paradise City
Return to the Madlands
The Mire Man: *The Complete Trilogy*
Lockless Doors in the Land of Harsh Angels
The Sounds From the Hills Go Away When the Sun Goes Down
No Old Souls At Fury Tavern

THE TWO REVOLVERS SAGA
Book I- Leave My Ashes on Blackheart Mountain
Book II- Legend of the Horizon Vengeance
Book III- MERCY

POETRY AND SHORT STORIES
The Kaleidoscope Syndrome: *An Anthology*
Wanderlust and the Whiskey Bottle Parallel: *Poems and Stories*
Strange Rainfall on the Rooftops of People Watchers: *Poems and Stories*
EJACULATION: *New Poems and Stories*
An Anvil of Night, A Hammer for Dawn: Poetry and Stories
On the Verge of Burning Down the Church: Poetry and Stories
Black Hibiscus: New Poetry
The Whores of Alcatraz: Poems 2007-2019
A Scorched and Mystified Wilderness: And Other Stories
A Cage for the Wind

SERIAL NOVELS
Woodbury Tabernacle: Volume One

Index of Poems

A CAGE for the WIND

"You develop an instant global consciousness, a people orientation, an intense dissatisfaction with the state of the world, and a compulsion to do something about it. From out there on the moon, international politics look so petty. You want to grab a politician by the scruff of the neck and drag him a quarter of a million miles out and say, 'Look at that, you son of a bitch.'"

— Edgar Mitchell, the sixth man to walk on the moon

"Astronauts are inherently insane. And really noble."

— Andy Weir, author of The Martian

"I thought the attractions of being an astronaut were actually, not so much the moon, but flying in a completely new medium."

– ***Neil Armstrong***

Telephone operator: *no sir, there is no one here by that name*

Jerry: *are you absolutely positive?*

Telephone operator: *yes, yes I am*

Jerry: *would you bet years of your life against it?*

Telephone operator: *Yes, for god's sake, yes*

Jerry started out like most of us
small
Childlike
A child, really, with all the facets that come with childhood
Imagination being chief amongst them
But one day, when Jerry was still very small
He watched
from the cracked door of the upstairs bathroom
his mother bathing alone in the porcelain tub
she had candles lit, none of which smelled like anything in particular but if they did, Jerry didn't have a word to put alongside those scents
she held aloft a glass of something clear, which he didn't know at the time to be vodka,
but it most certainly was vodka, straight up with no inclusions
her breasts were out of the water poking up
gooseskin coarsing over her exposed flesh
and she said to no one at all:
"I would just for once, like to wake up tomorrow, and be excited to be alive"
Jerry had an imagination fit for a child,
But his memory-keeping skills had not yet begun to really develop
and he forgot all about this shortly after

In the storybook Jerry favored most there were pictures of moons and stars and astronauts and space ships with faces painted on them
In the night, Jerry heard the sound of glass shattering, and the faint whimper of his mother sobbing over something she never spoke of to anyone

I: office/ psycho killer ?

Between the night spaces and wintertree branches, beneath the dirt crawlers and sleeping cricket noises, rest the bones of Jerry

Jerry, like most of us, was once alive, and not in the traditional sense of the word, because you see, "alive" can mean many things, or it can mean very few things, or, as it does moreoften than not, it can mean nothing at all

Jerry, had it very difficult growing up, though he'd be very hard-pressed to admit that to anyone even if they were being paid to listen to those stories

This story, the story of Jerry, is just one of many, as there are many of us wearing similar shoes to the ones Jerry fancies, and to some there may be nothing different about it, nothing new or ground-breaking

But that is fine,
All of that is fine
In the same sense that a fly does not care when it is smacked dead on the dashboard of a moving vehicle, Jerry would not care to be compared to any one or any thing
He is, or was, just a person like any other
Until, of course, something happened to change that

Not yet light outside

I already knew what it was like to not care from when I was young
But as I grew older I stopped caring about so much that I stopped realizing I'd done so
I didn't care that *I didn't care*
And it felt good
But what they don't tell you
Is that when you stop caring about
Enough things,
Enough matters,
Enough people,
You really start to feel the emptiness

Eventually you try to fill that emptiness
With anything you can,
Just to feel alive enough to *stay* alive
You try to fill that emptiness
With anything you can
And it doesn't matter who you may hurt in doing so

Your relaxing,
cloudy, windy, light-rainy spackled
autumn days
become violent,
And one day you wake up
And realize inspite of it all
You do care about something
Yourself

When I discovered my wife
had been having an affair, I couldn't masturbate
for three to four months,
which was frustrating since
it was something I still liked doing as an adult
I couldn't look at my cock without imagining someone else's
cock inside of *her*
I had to relearn how to not care, I'd been so good at it before
But when she climbed in bed with another man
That changed everything inside of me
She took away my ability to be apathetic
And I can't decide if I hated her more for that
Or for fucking another man
I tried remembering past women
The women of my youth were different, of course
Many of them were far more adventurous
I think because I had been the same way,
I used to want *more* from experiences than just
The experience
That's what got me hooked
Their spirit

Hannah had been like that
Thirty years ago
That's three decades
she sent through email a series of photographs,
in each of them she wore less and less
unbuttoning a blue and green flannel shirt
button by button

until finally she revealed her breasts
and the gash between her thick milky thighs

I had a swelling to deal with
Any urgency less than immediate would not do

I ran my hand over the form of my erection
And when it was over I told her about it
I said I never came so hard
She said it made her happy,
Honored

A week later her daughter came to me and said
"I think we should break up, I can't be with someone who
wants my mother as much as he wants me..."
There were more words than those,
And each of them hurt more than the ones that came before

That was only the start
The start
The beginning
I told myself to look forward to the end
Because moreoften than not
An end means another beginning

Thirty years later
I still remember how it felt to
ejaculate to her pictures
just her pictures
not on her face
or inside of her
something about it felt wrong
like I'd gotten away with murder

Thirty-one years following that night,
I'm in-
In the office,
The chairs all squeek and squeel
The management doesn't care about those kinds of sounds
They only care about profit
And phone time
And the cord that connects us to our phones

Outside most everyone smokes and so
Everyone's clothes smell like death

Back out in the office, my boss asks me why I'm leaving
He says the day isn't over yet
He says he's seen my numbers and I haven't been as productive as I was nine years ago
I tell him if he tries to stop me from leaving,
I'll look up his address in the company files and kick down his door one night
I'll kill him so good that it'll take all night
The asshole actually asks me if I'm being serious
I ask him why would I say something so horrible if I wasn't serious

The next day, the office called my boss's house,
The number he has on file
It seems he hasn't shown up to work
The phone just keeps ringing
No answer
No answer
No answer

In the bathroom, there's a man crying because he just found out he wouldn't be getting the raise he thought he would this year
Everything for him has just gone to shit
He says his kids already wear too much second hand clothing
And his wife doesn't remember the way his cock tastes anymore
I tell him that's maybe a good thing, and I tell him to remind her one night, to pick a night, to pull it out when it's hard and ready and even if it only lasts a minute, it'll let her know he still loves her

I say "women love to be reminded they are loved by seeing the cock they once thought they wanted for the rest of their life"
He says he's tried that already and she only ended up laughing
He says she took the opportunity to go out with friends and she stayed out all night
He says she never used to stay out all night

It's all new to him

And to his kids, their clothes are all old and the sports they play take up too much time to remember they have parents at all

To him it's new, to lose, and to be aware you're losing it

I say to him as I piss my last drops "it's okay to lose, I lost a lot and I'm still losing, you spend half of your life gaining, and the other half losing it all, at least I have, so that must mean others have it the same"

He locks the shitter stall door
He doesn't sit down to shit
He just keeps crying

Wind chime

The tune is soft
Like a breeze through high grass
You can't hear it
No one can hear it
But one day you wake up
And suddenly you know exactly how to start the day

There is a hum,
And you hum along until
You feel the absence
The absence is the real killer
You never did anything wrong
The world has its pockets of glass
Holes you fall into
Leading down into the stomachs of different beasts
We are all being digested over the course of our lives

Here, the voice is cast hardest
For what you are
What you can offer
It is grateful for the meal you have provided

Jerry has one vice
Telling lies
Lies are better than the truth, he often thinks to himself
To his coworkers, at the end of the day they envision him going home to a normal-looking wife,
She has a cooking book for every holiday, with different-colored sticky flaps sticking out to mark the best recipes, the ones she'll pass down to her children and hopefully their children,
(... "A woman's cookbook is her only sure path to her own immortality"...Jerry once heard that, and until his own mother died, he actually believed it...)
she knows how to walk from the stove to the refridgerator without forgetting to tuck in her elbows because one of the countertop edges is slightly uneven,
she waters the plants and asks her husband every day how his day was, even if it's just to fill the room with a sound other than aching silence
She has varicose veins running up and down her thighs and her calves,
And there's one really big one in the middle of her arm where the doctor's love to draw blood from,
Both of her breasts hang loose, one slightly lower than the other, about half an inch lower

Jerry speaks very minimally about his home life,
But his coworkers picture his wife as such because
Jerry is as normal-looking as one might imagine

To Jerry's coworkers,
He also has a son,
And his son once had a daughter,
But she was born with a hole in her heart and only one eardrum,
Not surprisingly, they didn't have the money to ensure a high-enough survival rate
But Jerry's son is still as happy as ever
He plays shortstop on a minor-league team,
He likes hockey more but knows his father grew up loving baseball,
So he wants to make his father as happy as he can
To Jerry's coworkers,
Jerry's springtime is full of cheers from the bleechers, and dust kicked up from sliding into home
And each night, he climbs into bed, kisses his wife on her head, and says he'll see her in the morning

Jerry is a liar

I opened the door and there he sat,
Right where I last left him
This damn cat

I started out hating him because he pissed in my garden out front enough to kill all the daffodils
But when the snowstorm of last year hit
I had to bring him in
He looked like he was going to die
I hated him, but that
Didn't mean I wished death on the poor beast

I call him Grimace
Because his teeth were so bad his lips would get stuck and when they got stuck, well,
He grimaced
So Grimace it was
And Grimace is still a son of a bitch
But for some reason, since last winter,
He thinks of me as his own
He sleeps in bed with me every night
He tells me when he's hungry
He watches me masturbate with that disappointing glare
He looks at me while I scrub my body in the shower
And when I step out of the shower,
He tells me about *his* day
This oftentimes involves him voicing what he thinks is a valid opinion
I'm not sure what that opinion is in reference to
I can only tell him I don't know what he wants
"I DON'T KNOW WHAT YOU WANT!" I'll say
I put more food on his plate and sometimes he eats it and sometimes he shits some more in his box
Grimace is a cultural asshole, the sum of every racial slur invented for the purpose of inflicting insult and pain
Sometimes I have dreams about waking up and he's gone,

Escaped in the night
Never to return
I'm not sad,
I just hope he's found happiness
But every morning I wake up and he's still there
Looking out the window
Like some bitch I'd fucked the night before expecting me to make her pancakes for breakfast

Grimace's remaining years

how this black and white son of a bitch
ended up with me
I'm not talking about how he got here,
I mean fate
The stuff all these astrologists believe in
To them he must've been a Virgo
And because I'm a Scorpio
Of course the stars were aligned in our favor
it's impossible to know
it's been a great year
I wonder how many the old man has left
he has less teeth than when he first walked in
and that's sayin' a lot

he finds ways to guilt us out of sex
not sex
masturbation
I can't shut the door on him
he'll break it down with his head
his tail twitches whether he's happy, sad,
or both happy and sad
his emotions are few
and he thinks that makes him saintly

and now that he has this tower
he's discovered new ways to send his judgments
he sits there at the top
the son of a bitch
the son
of a bitch

I wish he'd live forever
he deserves to, I think,
I wish there was a less likely chance in us
outliving him,
Us, people

he has years left, sure
but how many,

how many, old man?
You watch all the cars go by from your window,
you watch the birds and the woodpeckers and the-

how many years do ya have left?

I took off for the reunion
The high school reunion
My mother said, before she died, that I should go,
She said even if it's in vain
I'd be able to see how far I've come,
And how poorly everyone else has done
Our little town wasn't known for producing the heroes of the future
The most honorable mention, at least in the last fifty years, went to Wilson Pearl, a boy who spent as much of his high school career as possible in drama club, getting finger-banged by the varsity boy's wrestling coach, and finding new ways to voice his distaste with the cafeteria's lack of vegan options, all while sounding like he meant to save the civilized world from itself
I liked him because he always wore the best perfumes
They smelled like all the girls I ever wanted to fuck, but would never get the chance to
So I always tried to sit as close to him as I could if we ever shared a class together
In Music Theory 102, I could close my eyes, breathe in through my nose, mentally masturbate to the thoughts of one of the goths in those cool red and black plaid skirts, cum in my pants,
and clean up in the boys room before the bell rang without anyone ever noticing something had gone awry
All thanks to Wilson Pearl
He was a pearl, alright

Wilson Pearl
was a senior when I turned Sophomore,
He was killed in a car wreck two years after his graduation
Not sure what the cause was
Drunk driver maybe
His family was devasted

I remember the funeral, I went to the viewing to pay my re-
spects because he'd given me so much
The flower stands smelled like something he'd wear
That was the only day I ever shed a tear for the dead
The day Wilson Pearl was put into the ground

Out of respect, I didn't cum once that day
But at 12:01 the following morning
I impregnated the sky with a well thought-out gift

the friends

Dan left one day and never came back
no one heard from him again
I think he's in New York
the state, or the city,
I'm not sure

Lonny moved south and married rich
he's done something the media calls "impressive" with his body
and now wants to fight people for sport
He thanks God for everything,
but only when he wins a fight

Eric had some issues with his heart
and now I think he might be sober
I think he mighta got a new heart, too

Frank and I lived together for a few years,
but we haven't spoken in close to five;
and it's true-
you can't really truly know someone
until you live with them
He tried to fuck my wife,
and I think it's funny that I used to be mad about that

Melani didn't marry,
but now she's got two kids
and I think she likes the abuse,
but who can tell,
she's always smiling and trying new hair products

Linda looks happy with her kids and her husband,
I think she's the only one who actually *is* happy,
And I think she's the only one who deserves to *be* happy

Kendra has kids too, and a ring on her finger,
I used to kiss her hard and long on couches,
and stick my finger inside of her,
two fingers usually, sometimes three, sometimes four
Her cunt juice smelled good, untainted

James inspects buildings for toxic rot
Sam joined the Airforce and now he's set for life
Fred joined the Army and I think he's still in China,
or Okinawa
Matt went to the police academy just like his dad,
last I heard he's still a dumbass with sand between his toes,
but now with a badge on his chest

Garry was told by every teacher that they'd find him dead in
a ditch one day;
last year he was found dead by the edge of a river,
his body was frozen from the night cold
no one really knows why
His family didn't give him a funeral
They tossed his body in a hole and told his younger brother
now was his chance to shine

and I'm here writing these thoughts
they used to say I was the glue that held everyone together
they would say, "Jerry, if it wasn't for you, we all wouldn't be
together"
but I think everyone was held together because
together, we were *us*
we were together because we were together
that's it

and now they are all gone

but are they really gone
if all I am is the accumulation of their laughter?
memories of them are my memories
am I theirs?

we all keep going
until we don't anymore

The doors opened
The gymnasium smelled like wood scrub and
Club sandwich platters
There was also a punch bowl that Fred Jahima was pouring something into,
I heard during senior prom, he poured his own piss into it, but that wouldn't explain how everyone in their suits and dresses ended up as drunk as they did
I dipped my pinky into the punch bowl and tasted,
Fred was watching me
I said, not bad
He grinned, showing me his flask
I told him if it's his own piss that I'd murder him
I told him I killed my boss earlier that week,
So to kill him wouldn't be a problem
He told me I was a liar
I told him I didn't think he'd make it through the night with that attitude

Most of the girls, now women, were pregnant,
Or showing off their new skin,
Their new tits,
Their calf implants,
Their stomach pulls,
Their lips that looked like sausages
They all had astronauts for husbands
And what was I?
I told them I slept with a cat every night and had a career in office work
I got a lot of "oh, that's nice"'s and "that's interesting"'s and "I never thought that's how you'd end up"'s

I kept on the appearance of a man who doesn't really want to be there,
Maybe that would grab the attention of someone like me

Maybe we'd go home and they'd see my cat and see that I can commit to something
They're always saying that's a damn fine quality in a man

I drank a full glass of Fred's punch
And I suddenly had an idea
I should pick someone
and just start talking to them
anyone really
anyone might do
but what was I in the mood for?
I had to be strategic
I couldn't pick a married couple
They were *too* committed
I'd fuck up their vibe
And by extension, my own

After some time,
And three more helpings of Fred's punch,
I saw her
She was small,
Only just below my shoulders in height,
And she looked the same as I felt
She drank from a punch cup herself
And she took an extra long time to taste it before swallowing
My god, with a head of hair on her head
Red, like the fake kind you find in a box
She saw me looking at her and I could only imagine the revulsion, but she
Kept
Looking
Back
At me

Jerry was lost in terms of strategy,
So, he started off with a lie he once told his childhood guidance counsellor

Through conversation,
And through conversation meaning he spent the majority of the time listening to her talk rather than offer his own contribution,
He came to understand her name to be Iris

and Iris,
unbeknownst to Jerry,
knew that one way or another,
she was either going to fuck Jerry, or kill him

Iris seemed to be waiting for something although she didn't appear impatient
Jerry let her know that he had no intention of being coy with her
And she nodded, letting him know that she was appreciative of that
She said she'd grown too used to men who didn't know what they wanted out of life, and that if one more crossed her path, she might kill him for real,
She actually used the word 'murder' in a way that to Jerry, because he was quite familiar with its meaning, sounded too convincing to be untrue

Jerry didn't know what to say, he was sure she wasn't that similar to him, but those sorts of assumptions didn't matter, not yet at least

All he wanted was to have a conversation
He wanted to look like he belonged there
As though he meant to attend on his own accord
Despite the popular cliché, there were the select
few attending their high school reunions who
were genuinely interested in the goings-on in
their former classmates' lives and Jerry wanted to
be one of those people,
Or
at least
feel like it for the duration of the evening

This out-of-place redhead was his only shot out of
the entire gymnasium

After my mother died,
There birthed in her absence a void,
I was told most people go through a process,
Their own process and in most cases, it's healthy no matter
what that process turns out being
As long as they go through one
and come out on the other side

Years before Iris,
I once brought a girl to the cemetery,
We worked together,
Same store, different departments
She thought I was cute, I thought she was cute
I told her I knew a quiet place to go where we could have
sex,
And she didn't seem to care that the place ended up being
the cemetery
We went there three or four times a week,
She didn't care that I smelled like the seafood department
And I didn't care at all because she was the prettiest girl at
the grocery store
In the end,
Our demons didn't vibe for very long

My demons manifested into a black spot of toxic jealousy
and hers managed themselves into a long-winded plunge
into adulthood jaded by overbearing religious parents, and a
brother sent to jail for the attempted rape of his spouse

The morning after the high school reunion,
I took Iris to the same cemetery
I knew then that she was the one
Because she didn't ask why
She didn't ask anything at all

<u>of soulmates and calamitous fate</u>

The world here is cold,
everything feels coarse like
old autumn bark

we walk among the dead,
it is a dance many have danced
but few have danced to the end

in the black of night, we kiss,
in the crystaline dawn,
the land shucks off winter's husk
and furiously
our paths abandon,
whittling into tangled strands of longing and
opaque, barren, hypotheses

we won't meet again,
this newness we share,
after this, everything will begin to grow old
nothing will ever be this good

It was New Boss Day at the office,
And this time
He was a hobbit named Gus Tideman
He said it was important to start off new relationships with fond memories of childhood awkwardness
He said when he was a kid,
His nick name was Tidy Tideman because
He was afraid of anything dirty
Kid Gus was so afraid of dirty things he would fall onto the floor and curl himself into the tightest ball that he could,
He would shiver and wimper and kick anyone who tried to untangle him
He hated things like mud, the dirt form of mud, he hated using the school bathrooms, he hated using the trays in the cafeteria, he even hated things like shoelaces and velcro because he felt that those were the sorts of things that attracted and collected the most dirt

But Tidy Tideman had grown into a man of reflection and self-aware humor, he said
And he thought that we should all take part in his regime, to better get to know one another
As if we hadn't been working with each other for the last decade
He said there was a cloud hanging over the office and he meant to part that cloud
With what, I didn't know
Sunshine maybe
Maybe he thought he was God
Maybe he really was God
He made us write on a piece of paper one awkward childhood memory
Jane, the receptionist, said she had a thing for little Bobby Wilmot even though his braces actually worsened his dental situation

Pete Heins apparently didn't know second base was mandatory when running to third one day, so he skipped it and the boys in his class that year never let him forget about it, even bullying him into contemplating suicide; in high school though he was among the first to make it to second base in a significantly different way, which earned him a new, more respectable reputation amongst the more renowned hallway whores

Kenneth Burrows opened his lunch bag one afternoon and found that the banana inside had fully depreciated not only its nutritional, but also its consummatory value; the bully two grades above saw it as another opportunity to make Kenny's penis seem even more impure than the going theory

There were more stories and most everyone seemed to enjoy it,
I don't recall the office ever being as loud with laughter as that morning
Gus Tideman was already on his way to being a
More-enjoyed boss than the last,
Even I could see the appeal
But something was off about him
No one is ever this great on their first day

That afternoon he was making the rounds
No self-respecting boss ever made "rounds"
When he reached my desk he asked why I didn't participate in the activity earlier
Said I was the only one who opted out
I told him my childhood wasn't akward, it
Was not very interesting at all
Tidy Tideman didn't seem to believe me
But he spoke like a guidance counsellor
"I don't think that's ever true of anyone," he said, folding his arms and leaning against the south-most partition of my

cubicle, "you just haven't figured out a way to tell your story that others can latch on to."

I thought about Iris then
I thought maybe she might find some of my childhood memories interesting,
But since our last meeting,
I gathered she wasn't one to really hinge a relationship on the childhood foundation of its spouses
Iris stood on a mountain of past,
You could see it in the way she didn't speak at times other people normally might,
You could feel it in the manner in which the air around her changed as she breathed,
But she didn't care about it
Her past hadn't molded her in the same way a politician might use as a platform for presidential election
To Iris, the past was the past, and had no correlation to the present or the future
To Iris, the past, the present, and the future,
were three separate entities,
Three areas of thought,
Three sentences in three separate books resting on three entirely separate bookshelves in houses built on three different contintents

Gus Tideman said he wanted a childhood memory that affected the way I matured into an adult, written on a piece of paper and placed on his desk by the end of the day
Before I could ask for his opinion about murder in the workplace, he'd wandered off to shoot the shit with Jane to talk about which of her desktop plants were her favorite

Jerry sharpened a pencil with the kind of sharpener you have to crank your hand with in a grinding motion
He chose to write with a pencil because he wanted to be sure he'd have the chance to correct any mistakes he most certainly would make during the writing process
Jerry was not a writer, he knew
He was a liar, which he also knew
He figured there must be some correlation between the two, that writing must depend on the author's ability to lie
He knew even before he decided against using a pen, that his childhood was not interesting enough even to embellish
So he began with a lie he'd used once before during a slightly different situation involving the first date with his first not-at-all real wife

Jerry wanted to convey a feeling of childhood authenticity to his new supervisor,
So he chose to write his little lie on a piece of lined paper torn from a wirebound, three-hole-punched notebook, the same kind of notebook he used from grades four to eleven
He made sure to tear the paper out in a way that the frilly fringe stayed on the edge of the page
Because
He was very careless as a child when it came to such practices
Ripping a piece of paper from its notebook along the dotted line was not one of Jerry's more prominent talents

In fact, the habit formed when he realized it was a reliable way to annoy his teachers, an act of rebellion which would blossom into more psychologically-violent acts during his high school career

Jerry's first wife, the one before the woman with varicose veins and naturally uneven breasts, according to the lie, was Agnes Elizabeth Roberts, her sister was obsessed with fingernail polish, foreign beauty routines, and other obscure cosmetological schools of thought,
but Anges,
she went to school to become a librarian specifically due to her love of books, and therefore wanted to dedicate her life to caring for them

Agnes was a fiend for the written word,
She relished reading during every free moment she could muster, and in doing so strained her eyes, forcing her to be prescribed a pair of glasses at the age of thirty-three, which, not entirely central to the story, were thick, black-rimmed glasses her eye doctor said was all the rage amongst librarians

When Jerry met Agnes, she'd been cataloging a newly-published update of the first five Nancy Drew novels,
She'd been muttering something to herself about her disliking of the abandoning of the series' traditional yellow spine, making the books, in her opinion, seem less genuine

He noticed the way her hair was tied behind her head and in doing so became, at that particular time in his life, uncharacteristically distracted,
he tripped over the heel of her shoe and fell all the way down to the floor
If the floor had been any harder, he might have cracked his skull open

Agnes felt so bad she bought him a coffee from the shop across the street,
She said she was so embarassed and so very sorry,
It was there Jerry told her about the time he was going to church, specifically the day of his First Holy Communion,
For some reason, as opposed to every other day he'd worn them, Jerry put his dress shoes each on the wrong foot,
To be fair he was still very young, and those shoes looked so very much alike it was honestly hard to tell the right apart from the left,
They were so alike in shape and appearance, they could very well be mistaken for the opposite foot one was meant for
And so, in failing to successfully differentiate the proper orientation, he walked down the great aisle of Saint Joseph's Catholic Church, taking his turn to receive the honorable sacrement of the Lord's approval,
It wasn't until Eric Langston stepped aside so that Jerry could take his turn, that Father Lewis' exceptionally keen eyes caught sight of the possessed child in front of him,
And it was true to the extent of his knowledge,

Jerry's misplaced footwear made him appear as though he were a child possessed by an actual demonic spirit sent straight from the deepest depths of Hell by Satan himself,
He walked strangely and wore a look of worry, not stalwart godliness the High Almighty looked for when bestowing upon his children sacrements of endorsement into adulthood

At the sight of Jerry,
Father Lewis choked on his own saliva,
Dropped the silver platter of little round holy communion piece of bread,
And uttered out a slew of perfectly-pronounced swear words that echoed through the entire church,
The audience, the mothers and fathers of those children in their little white gowns and suits, sat in disbelief, calcified in terror, gasping while others fainted

Jerry stood enraptued by his own shock,
Young and not knowing at all how to react,
While the normally composed and, frankly terrifying, Father Lewis writhed in an attempt to clear his own throat
When Father Lewis could finally stand,
The church had fallen silent, and the truth of his outburst suddenly ascended to the forefront,
And there Jerry stood, still waiting for his piece of holy communion bread

That was the story Jerry told Agnes, and Agnes laughed so hard that laughter eventually evolved into love for the man
It was also the lie Jerry wrote about on that lined piece of frilly notebook paper and turned in to Gus Tideman at the end of the day
Gus laughed at the end of reading it and said
"See, wasn't so hard, was it?"
Jerry played it cool, or so he thought
But Gus was on to him
Gus knew about his poor numbers
Gus Tideman was on to all of the office workers

On our second date,
Iris did the taking-out

She took me to a comedy club,
"The Neon Winnebago", she called it
The Neon Winnebago was a classy joint without all the class
Most of its patrons wore flannels and beanies
the men styled their beards expensive, scented moisturizers
and their women
Wore music on their shirts
I ordered a double
And made a shape with my hand
My two fore fingers on one top of the other
The waitor nodded with a thumbs up and a
"classy choice, I like your style"
Iris said she'd have a dark beer

All was nice
The lights were low and no one cared that I lit a cigarette
But about thirty minutes in after we sat down and we had
our drinks,
I had to ask her why no one else besides me was laughing
Turns out it was a poetry reading,
And everyone here
Were poets
Not a single comedian in the house
Nothing to laugh at
Everything to cry over and
Reminisc
Things they couldn't change
Society
Society
Society
The government
Oppression
Working-class back-patting

The cunt that got away, without calling her a cunt
The girl who stayed but sucked the life out of the room
The wife
The daughter
The father
The son
The grocery store clerk
And his secret identity as a moonlighting alcoholic
And they all loved jazz
LOVED it

Iris asked if I was enjoying myself
I said sure, she was there
and I had a pretty good drink
What's not to enjoy?
But I think she was talking about the poetry
I told her I've never really touched poetry much
Or reading
I wasn't into the arts like some people
This seemed to offend her
Most of the color had left her cheeks
And her lips didn't seem to absorb the beer she drank the way they did when she was smiling
And for the very first time
I felt like I was losing her

with flame in the hearth, her legs quivered

Breathe
a harsh tone abroad the outreach
there's help coming
but
what does it look like?
Does it have a face?
Does she have a name?
Is she coming over at sunset
Or just before the cold dawn?

A train rolls in and the night air screeches
She's here at last
I can hear her taking those iron steps
Down to the street
Under the thin street lamp glow
She looks changed
I don't recognize her
I call out to her anyway
Maybe there's still hope
But my timing is off
As the train pulls away
All she hears are the tracks
And for the first time
I feel like I never knew her

She wanders towards me, her skin white
The clothes have gone,
crumpled in directionless heaps of discarded snakeskin
She doesn't shiver though it's snowing
And snowing hard
She has changed
I don't recognize her
I take her home
But the warmth behind these walls
She doesn't like it
It's odd, she says
It's an odd thing to feel this way
She says's she's changed
And only now does she realize
That I have stayed the same

Jerry felt that his time with Iris would end soon, and so he decided it would be best in the grand scheme of things, being the grand scheme of the world and the universe, to get the separation over and done with, out of the way, scratched from the list, packed up and sent away, "fingered and bottled", as his father would say, or, "plucked and chucked", as his grandfather would, so that he could move on with his life and she could find someone or something that would compliment her edges more properly

Jerry found this task to be rather difficult, however, as the day after the boring comedy show at The Neon Winnebago, Iris was nowhere to be found. She wouldn't answer her phone calls, which was odd in and of itself being she was usually the one to call Jerry

Jerry thought about calling in sick, but realized that would depreciate his own spiritual value. If he called in sick, that would mean he actually cared about Iris in a way that frankly, sickened him. So he went to work as he usually did

When he arrived, Gus Tideman was just about to give his morning encouragements to the "troops" as he called them...

Gus stood outside of his office with a hand on each of his hips
His lips curled up and down as though he were just about to give the greatest speech of his life
That's when I walked in
Just in time to punch the clock before being what was commonly thought of as being "unnacceptably late"

I found my desk and slumped down hard enough to make the legs holding up my desk jiggle
It was around that time I noticed something different
Different is not always good
Different can sometimes be very, very bad

The monsters are here

Beth,
If that is her name
Wore a snout like a halloween prop
She was a pig with great big nostrils who no one wanted to marry but everyone wanted to fuck

Henry,
Laid on his desk
Like an insect with its head bitten off

And Harold,
Was eating Henry's head,
Chewing,
With great, big, hideous insect jaws

Mary Lou,
Mary Lou,
Where do I begin with you
She was tall in life
But I suppose now that she had turned into a giraff
Nothing much had changed for her

Two grinning monkeys rolled around in the far corner fucking each other
I don't even know their names

What was today?
Today was not Monday
It was not Tuesday
It was not the anniversary of any known holiday
And my birthday isn't for another three months
What was today?

Gus returned his attention to the rest of the team
His "troops"
"Troops!" He cried out
"Production has been, dwindling, BUT, I still have faith in you all. It's not quite time that we'll have to look closer at the numbers to see who goes and who stays, BUT, I just wanted you all to know that I know you are all working hard. But working hard is not always the best one can work, is it? Of course not. Working hard is simply the minimal effort!"
And then
"Jerry, my office, now!"
And then he gave everyone else a thumbs up and
I got up from my desk

He told me to shut the door
I shut the door and noticed his face
It was very hurried
Whatever reason he brought me in for, he wanted to say it quickly so he could get out with... whatever

"Jerry," he started
"You're firing me."
"Hells no," he laughed, "sit down, look, wait no, those blinds behind you, close them."
As I closed the blinds, Gus removed from his desk drawer a bottle of gin
"I'm more of a whiskey guy," I said
"I know, the gin is for me," he said as he pulled out from the drawer a bottle of whiskey
"You're a strange guy, Gus," I said, taking from him the glass he'd just filled
I smelled the whiskey
It was sharp
Hot
Burning and spicy

The heat would probably burn the nose hairs out of a thirteen year old's nose
"I'm only strange to the normal people. Are you normal?"
I drank the whiskey in one mouthful
Before Gus could grab the bottle, I grabbed it,
And refilled my glass
"This stuff burns like a bonfire," I said
I looked at the label
It read:
"Bonfire Tears"
"I know," Gus replied, "I like it too,"
"So what's the meaning of all this?"

Gus sipped his gin carefully,
Very small mouthfuls,
His lips became soaked with the stuff and
Glistened
Like
Snowfall

"I'm taking a adhesive company to court next month," Gus said, "my daughter's elementary school purchased a whole new assortment of glue for the students, the art classes, things like that. Well, they went with this new company, Alabaster's Plasters, or something, that's famous for offering alternative products to whatever's most popular. Their catch this year is a new line of glue that's, get this, gluten free. Apparently their designers took into consideration just how many young kids in the lower grades eat the stuff and figured why not poke another hole in their belt. Well, my daughter was apparently allergic to one of the additives in said glue and she had an attack. Yea. Neck swelled up like a papaya. She's fine, she's fine. But I'm taking this sycophantic Alabaster's Plasters to court because no one gets away with almost killing my daughter with gluten free glue. Anyway, I'm going to have to be out of town for a while. And I need someone to man the fort until I get back."

At first,
Jerry didn't know what to think
The idea that Gus Tideman may in fact actually be mad was no longer a joke in his mind
Responsibility greater than the boundaries of his desk was the last thing Jerry ever wanted, even if it meant a raise
The desk was his safe space, it was a dugout in which he never had to come out from
But now his boss was asking him to pinch-hit
And Jerry was not at all a fan of the idea

Jerry knew,
That under his leadership
The office would burn to the ground in a matter of hours

Jerry looked at Gus
Gus looked at Jerry
Both of them were two glasses in to their favorite beverage of choice

I sat on my couch
Grimace was still waiting for me to feed him
He looked at me with those yellow eyes
Diamond cut eyes in a mine of black dread
On the coffee table there was my ashtray
Filled with ash and six or seven crinkled butts
A shot glass
A full-sized whiskey glass
A half-drunk bottle of Red's Turnpike Whisperer
A notebook with phone numbers of people I used to know written inside
A two-foot long receipt from Big Cheap Market
And the keys to the office,
Two gold-plated, one-inch long pieces of metal with short teeth and short noses
They were both slung on a ring and there was
Something
Weird
About them
They felt light when in my pocket
But when I held them
Their weight become more
Ubiquitous

I found Iris, finally
She was sitting on one of the more respectable stools at the bar on the corner of Turtle Street and Carver Avenue
By respectable,
I mean from the angle in which you walked in through the front door,
you couldn't see her cleavage or her cunt if she had been wearing a skirt with no clam shams
It'd been raining mixed with a little snow,
So when I walked in,
I must have looked like a monster covered in cold dust
And when she turned to see who it was who just walked in,
It sounded like thunder booming

But really
It was just the
nine o'clock route C bus bottoming out from those damn
potholes on Carver Avenue again

Iris looked surprised to see me
You'd think she'd been plotting my murder
And thought she'd never see me again

"I had a feelin' you'd be here," I muttered, "skankin' up the
joint, the whores always come back to the scene of the
crime," I really didn't mean to sound that mean,
sometimes it just comes out that way

Iris was sitting in her stool
But the stool next to her was being used by a man who even
from here
Smelled like an italian meat sandwich
He didn't look pleased
He must have thought I was her husband
In another time, perhaps, I could have been
"Why are you angry?" she asked
It was an honest question from the mouth of a dishonest
woman
"We made no pact," she said

She was right
I had no reason to be angry
She was doin' her thing
And I suppose all I could do was my own thing
Iris went on with her night
Drinking and talking to the guy in the stool next to her
I went home
And opened a new bottle of Tuesday Night Frequency

How much whiskey is too much?

How much is too much
How much is not enough

The night reaches a point
We all know it
The stretch marks streak across the sky
They
Linger
For a moment longer
And then suddenly
We are awake
Inside a new dream
Touching a new woman's thigh

You've had too much,
The doc says the morning after
Luckily,
you were with someone who cared about you,
they cared enough to bring ya here
they aren't here anymore,
they've had to go on with their day

The hospital walls begin to crack
And through the splitting fissures
She returns to the fold
The book closes
And morning welcomes afternoon

Drink more water,
You haven't had enough
You need to wash the toxicity from your insides
But I don't want to
I want to feel every
Waking
Moment
I want to know that I am dying
That this is the end

This is not enough
You've had too much
When the night comes back,
You won't be who you were yesterday

Grimace was eating something off the floor
It didn't take long for my sight to fix itself
He was chewing on something solid
Next to him was a pile of my own vomit that'd spent the night working itself into the carpet
Now it was nothing more than a crust
And Grimace thought I'd left it for him

"That's right buddy," I said, "it's all for you, all this vomit."

I lay sprawled on the floor not far from the vomit
I was also naked
The hair on my testicles stuck to the cum just beneath me, from when I'd cum in my sleep sometime in the night
Well,
My pants were gone
At some time in the night
I'd attempted to masturbate, I suppose
But either I passed out before I could finish
Or I finished and then I passed out

I rolled over onto my side until my back touched against the legs of the coffee table
Grimace chewing on my vomit
I picked the clumps of dried cum from my testicle hair until most of them were out
Then I scratched the side of my cock,
The side that had the three or four thick black hairs growing out of it like Hellsnakes
And then I adjusted my sack so that it didn't feel so neglected

"You're lucky, buddy," I said to Grimace, "you're lucky you don't have any of these emotions, like us people do. All you have to worry about is, well, in your case you don't have to worry about much. I think I take care of ya pretty well. I feed ya every day, tell you nice things, most of which are true. Even now, you look like a great cat. Mouthful of vomit, sure, why not. We've all been there, I suppose."

Outside
The universe shifted course
The sky was blue, yes,
But I could see the universe
The sky was not alone
It was not empty but filled with all the things everyone else cannot see
Ripples and tangents
Moons and spinning molten planet cores
Hot and cold creating steam and new elements
The universe itself is a cold place
But on the surface,
It is a swirl of so many warm colors
Twisting vines entangled in stars and flashes
A spinning free fall into and out
Outside the clouds met with the blue of the sky
And somewhere between
thought and understanding
I blinked away last night's melancholy

I twirled the keys to the office in the forefinger of my left hand
And in my right hand I held the day's paper
I never read the paper seriously
But I wanted to look the part
I wasn't sure if Gus had told anyone else about his plans
I know I wasn't as
Motivating
As Gus
But, I could at least look as though I cared
Appearances run the world but only those looking are unaware of this phenomenon

My head swelled with a thick fog as I unlocked the office door
Everyone around me were waiting
I was late, you see
Apparently the manager of the office always comes in early, before everyone else
They all wore frowns and uncharmed hatred
But also
Confusion
They must have been wondering where Gus was
"Killed another boss, did ya," Henry asked as I turned the key
He was joking
There's no way he could have known about...
"He's away for a while," I said, "I didn't kill him, I promise. He'll be back in due time. Fighting a case against Alabaster's Plasters."
It sounded like something someone intelligent might say
"What the hell is Alabaster's Plasters?"
"Some glue company, I don't know," I replied

In the office, the industrial heating roared to life and everyone took their places and I
Didn't know if I should take my usual spot
Or dip into Gus's throne room
The manager's office looked so snug and inviting
The second key on the key ring Gus had given me
Was the key for his office
Why would he give me the key to his office if he didn't mean for me to go in?

I unlocked it and walked into the scent of pine needles
And bergamot
"Hmm," I said, "Anges' favorite candle scent"
I'd stepped into this office many times
But only just now noticed the window on the far wall looking out into the trees down below

The trees
And the cemetery lying beyond
What luxury
It almost made the idea of *being* the manager enticing
I could never hold the throne for long, however
I wasn't the management type
Gus was the type to lead armies into the pointy spears of even bigger armies while maing his troops believe their were dying courageously for a good cause
I was the sort of guy to
Fuck Gus's wife, if he had one
Come to think of it, I wondered
Was Gus married?
I didn't know much about him other than the fact that he had a daughter
But was he still married?
Unimportant right now
Right now, it was time to run the office
And show these people who's boss

Just before lunch
Wilson, first name Neville,
Knocked on the door to Gus's office
Wilson was a short man, born with short legs
And long arms
He never grew above most anyone else's shoulders
Wilson didn't strike me as a father's son, mostly because most of the framed pictures in his cubicle were of him alongside an older lady whom he referred to as "mother"
Not mom
Just "mother"
He was a ginger
And in many places, that meant trouble
But in this office he'd carried himself as a meak, tender, sometimes overly shy individual with little to nothing to say about anything more than the weather

Whenever it snowed he made this little shivering motion with his shoulders and said "burrrr" while looking out a window
I think he was in accounting
But I didn't know what that meant because I wasn't in accounting and didn't know a goddamn thing about accounts receivable

He stood in the doorway waiting for me to tell him it was okay to enter
"Enter," I said, trying to sound like a strong, well-endowed manager who cared but instead the word emerged like it was being spoken by the fucking wizard of Oz
Wilson tiptoed in, the fingers of his hands interlinked
"How's the therapy coming along," I asked him

Wilson suffered from seasonal depression
During one of the holiday parties several years ago, he was found in the supply closet with a piece of glass
He looked to have been just about to slice open his wrists
The manager at the time, some misplaced Jew named Roger, implored him to seek help, and so he did
And as far as I knew, Wilson had been better for it

"He said I should find a new therapist," Wilson replied, "I'm not sure if that means I'm a particularly hard case, or if my current therapist is retiring, or what. It's all very confusing right now. My wife thinks I should have shopped around more before picking him out. It's so very difficult to decide on who's best to listen to your thoughts."
"Yes," I said, "I suppose that's true. It's not like picking out a car at the car lot. But anyway, how can I help ya?"
"Before Mr. Tideman left, he said he'd approved some time off for me next week, but in the schedule it doesn't reflect that. I was wondering if you could check that out for me."
"Well," I looked at Gus's computer, the manager's computer. The screensaver showed an image of some lake in another

country surrounded by foreign mountains capped with snow and ice, and the sky was embued with hues of pinks and purples. At the bottom of the screen in big bold white letters it read: “Opportunity”, finished off by some small-printed quote from the King James version of the Holy Bible

“I’m sure he must’ve given you all of his passwords for such an occasion,” Wilson filled in the blanks with his own logic

“Honestly I’m not really sure,” I said, “I’ll have to do some research and get back to ya on that. But honestly, if the guy approved it and he said it was fine, then I wouldn’t worry about it. Just don’t come in those days, no worries.”
Wilson’s expression brightened and he nodded, leaving shortly thereafter

I looked at the picture on Gus’s desktop that read “Opportunity” for a long time
“Being the boss isn’t so hard,” I muttered to myself

Jerry spent most of the following week answering the requests of his employees in much the same fashion
An employee whom either had a familiar face or a familiar name would come into Gus's office,
Voice a concern
And Jerry would wave them off telling them some version of the phrase "do what you want"
And so they did
Jerry expected Gus Tideman to call him periodically, or at the very least, in a very business-like fashion, email him
But there was nothing
And eight days after Gus Tideman left Jerry in charge, Jerry finally began to worry...

A hail of kidney stones

The body of a man hung in the closet
Strung up around his neck by a bootlace that'd once been advertised for hikers and extreme outdoorsmen
To his right,
There hung a suede jacket one might wear to a brunch shared with a beautiful woman
To his left,
remained a coathanger covered in a hundred different-colored neck ties
Here is a man having found the final purpose
There was denial, yes
I know someone else had done this
I was not responsible
This was too cruel a thing for me to do

I pushed the dead man aside and stepped in through the dark
The voice said to me "come in, come in"
I asked it, "Do you know why *he's* here?"
The voice said, "we have all the answers, all of them and more"

The bones came first
Falling down like rain
Behind them fell a shower of kidney stones,
Like hail,
Each one felt like a stone,
And when the hailstorm passed me by
I came to it at last,
The mountain
And beyond the mountain there lay a sky,
Accented with hues of pinks and purples
And entangled within those hues,
I thought I saw it
The answer
She came crawling through the blinds
And rolled out onto the floor
She was naked
Like a newborn
A new idea
A life ahead of her full of possibilities

But the mountain swallowed her
And I was back in my bedroom
The closet was now locked
And there was nothing I could do to open it

Jerry woke up in his bed
It was fifteen days since his boss gave him the responsibility of watching over the office
And it was three days since Gus Tideman had officially been declared missing
Thankfully,
Jerry knew for a fact he was innocent of anything related to his disappearance
He'd had a particularly terrifying and disconcerting dream prompting him to look under the bed, turn out all the closets, and investigate every vent in his apartment
There were no body parts
No blood stains
No signs of having hidden anything or stashing away incriminating evidence pointing to him as the perpetrator
The only thing that concerned him was that he still held the keys to the office
Unfortunately, Jerry was the last person to have had contact with Gus Tideman
And that made him a suspect
A suspect of what, he found himself wondering
He'd told the questioning authorities of Gus Tideman handing him the keys and the reason for which he was leaving
The authorities were very good at not giving away if they believed him or not
And so they only offered Jerry a static, apprehensive, and rather threatening: "don't leave town"
The threat was domineering, to say the least

Jerry didn't remember a time in his life he'd felt so afraid
So, of course,
He left town
And started anew
At first, Jerry started small
He left town
Bringing only Grimace
And some of Grimace's food
He left his belongings with the intention of one day returning because
In his honest opinion, he just might
He left the office keys on Gus Tideman's desk on a Saturday, so that no one would see him do so
And then,
He was off on the road
But as with anything else with a lifespan,
Circumstances evolved
And when simply "leaving town" became insufficient
he left the state altogether,
and ideas of returning to his home became syonymous with lifelike dreams fading from memory

Jerry was off on the road, Grimace close to the hip, and nothing but the pavement to tell him which way to go or otherwise...

Out of Town, Out of Sight

I found the keys to the road
And did what I'd done many times before
Before
"Before" is such a vast word,
No matter what context it's used in

I couldn't remember the last time I'd done this
The road does that to you
It takes your memory
And gives you a new one
And when the sun sets and rises
More and more
The old you breaks apart and
Soon you're someone else
I've done this many times before
That's the only truth
Like a cloud

I came to a new town
I met some new people
As before
I saw that the road kept going
But I didn't want to keep going
This place was far enough away from "before"
I could start new here
Everything that came before
Could stay where it was
I have all I ever needed

Where have all the bodies gone?

Where have all the bodies gone,
since the dawn of time?
For thousands of years we've lived and died
Billions of us
billions of faces and minds and loves and bad decisions
But where have all the bodies gone?
They cannot all be here,
they cannot all be under our feet
Are they stuffed into a rocket ship and blasted off
to the moon?
Is the moon's core filled with the skeletal remains of us?
Is that what we are destined for?
Where have all the bodies gone?
To the moon?
Someone should find out for sure
Someone is lying to us

II: hotels/ the great paralization

Something for no one

It's not always whiskey for me
Or even coffee
Sometimes it's tea
Black tea with honey
It's warm like a drinkable sweater
She had a big black pussy like someone had kicked her in the cunt with a size 19 boot
I went down on that big black pussy
Against my better judgment
And she moaned like a water buffalo
She had horns like one too
The hotel manager called
telling me to turn the tv down
I told him I had my hard white dick inside
Some big black pussy
And
he said he doesn't allow any blacks in his hotel
I told him she was white
Whiter than me
She only had a big black pussy
It was her pussy that was black, not the rest of her
He said to call him in the morning
He's got a good doc, he says
I told him sure
Sure thing
In the morning after Frenchetta left
I called the front desk
But the hotel manager wasn't there
I said is this a joke
My dick is on the line, here
The man at the front desk said he didn't care
No one cares
It's my fault
And next week, my dick will grow mushrooms
All up and down the shaft
The head will turn purple
Real purple
Like on the color spectrum
So bright

Everyone will be able to see it
And I'll remember Frenchetta,
Beautiful face
Great mouth
Big black pussy

I ordered three eggs over easy,
white toast and two sides of bacon,
soft and greasy if possible
but crispy if it wasn't possible

The bacon came out crispy
The orange juice arrived in a short glass and the coffee was poured into a white mug with a handle stained almost as brown as the coffee
The waitress who took my order and brought everything out had killer cleavage, I thought,
and her chest probably smelled good at least before she clocked in
Where she came up short was at her face
Resembling a used, pushed-in catcher's mit,
even her expression appeared used-up
Without so much as a faked grin,
her face was nothing more than a relic stored away in some hoarder's attic only taken out of its box to be remembered,
though probably not very fondly
This waitress though,
still had some use in her
She had a mean writing hand,
and the talons on her other grabber while holding the order pad would frighten an eagle
The way her wrist bent while wielding that blue ink pen, she could kill anyone or anything
in less than a second,
and if they survived, well,
that face of hers would surely finish them off

I scraped the plate clean of all its eggy contents with the last corner of white toast and took the rest of the orange juice down my throat
The waitress swung by one more time to drop off the check
and on the check I saw she'd written her name in messy cursive

"Jan," I said out loud.
"Short for January," she said
"Nine dollars and seventy-three cents," I said, "you didn't charge me for the coffee."
"It's not good enough to charge people for," Jan shrugged
"I didn't think it tasted all that bad," I said
"You're kind."
"I'm honest."
"Well, you can either pay at the register up front or I can take it from ya."
I stuffed a hand into my right pocket and handed her a wrinkled-up twenty. She held it and felt the green paper with her fingertips.
"I'll bring back your change."
"Keep it," I said, grabbing my keys off the table as I stood up.
"That's an awfully big tip, mister," she stopped on her way to the register
At the table next to her, a large man in a beige hardback hooded coat looked up from his mug of not-good-enough coffee and gave her a good look up and down
He nodded to his buddy sitting across from him.
"I'd slip it into her, maybe even shove it," he snickered
His buddy nodded along,
cutting into his waffle on his plate with loud scrapes of his knife and fork
Jan side-eyed them,
but shrugged it off quickly
I felt like saying something to the guy in the hardback coat, but he was a much bulkier man than I was
He had worker's hands, and I did too but not from working, his were from harder tools and longer shifts
mine were from obligation and necessity

I was a carboard box next to him, and he could crush me
like one.

"You're workin' your ass off," I said to her, "I've seen you workin' the other tables on top of mine. You haven't stopped all night. I'd give ya more of a tip but that's the last of my cash, and my card is in the truck."
"Oh," she waved the check around, "don't worry about it. Thank you, though. It's unusual for someone to be that generous around here."
I grabbed my coat and slipped my arms into the sleeves, stretching my fingers and cracking a few knuckles once they were through and out on the other side
I walked past the two gentlemen who'd commented about Jan
One of them smelled like something rotting
but I couldn't tell if it was one of them or
both of them

"Heh, big tipper," the one in the hardback coat muttered
with a mouthful of soupy scrambled eggs
I stopped by the door
I saw myself in the mirrored doorframe and imagined what
I could do to the man if I had more strength,
if I wasn't lanky in the arms and thin around my waist
Underneath my clothes,
My body consisted of some muscle,
but only enough to get me through basic motions, getting up
out of bed in the morning to get to work,
and then to climb back into bed after
I had almost no work-out regime,
and so I had no business confronting this monster of a man

I smiled at Jan on my way past the front register and pushed
my way out the door

I sat in my truck for a while, calming the nerves and taking a few breathers before getting back out on the road

These days
I drove a box truck for Municipal Supply, delivering bulk toiletries to schools, hospitals, municipal buildings, and sometimes, although it was extremely rare, shopping malls

Municipal Supply had its own fleet of over-the-road tractor trailers but to save money on paying all their employees as CDL-holding drivers, they kept on the books two or three small commercial truck drivers to handle the weekend work

That was where I existed

Now,
I worked
Friday's,
Saturday's,
and Sunday's,
driving a small box truck from customer to customer
It wasn't a huge truck,
which is why I took the job
I was a coward, I guess, but I didn't care about that, and I never told anyone that I was, so no one that I ever met knew

The smaller the truck,
the better

That being said,
this piece of shit handled like a son of a bitch
A slight breeze, particularly southbound on Delaware's route 1 stretch, would demand that I hold onto the wheel with both hands as tightly as I could, just so I could keep the damn thing on the road
The job wasn't my ideal place of employment,

But given the turn of events of days long passed, there
wasn't much that could be ideal

The job paid the bills and afforded me the more-than-occasional luxury of taking my breaks at any roadside diner I came across
Cheap, but delicious food
A tabletop jukebox to pick your favorite tunes to eat alongside of
And usually a waitress with great tits and a snappy attitude to bring you your meal
Once you walked through that silver-mirror door, the world outside disappeared entirely
You were in truck-stop heaven
A break was more than just a break from work,
it was a step into an entirely different world
Sitting down at the table alone,
you could share a moment with yourself,
and share a thought with no one.

I parked far-enough away from the diner so that I could see everything
I sank back in the driver's seat,
listening to a jazz station at low volume
Jazz had been new for me
Never before had I really paid much attention to it,
But I suppose that now,
These days,
With work on the road,
And Grimace waiting for me at home,
Jazz was a kind of company that loved from afar

I never knew whose music was playing,
but it was slow and smooth enough to match the descent of the orange sun to the west
Ahead, the man in the hardback coat and his buddy lumbered out of the diner like a pair of grizzlies

I couldn't hear them but they were laughing at something
They made their way back to their pickup truck, a forest green Ford something or other, slamming their doors after climbing in
The man in the hardback coat stomped onto the gas after shifting into gear, peeling out the tires and kicking up gravel as they merged out onto the road and sped off into the distance
I never saw them again,
but I'm almost positive one or both of them must have died in a fiery wreck of their doing

I must have fallen asleep behind the dash, as when I woke up the sky was completely black and the diner lights were all alight with neon greens and pinks and purples
In one of the windows had been set the neon outline of a mountain range, capped in white neon luminescence
Through the radio,
whoever was talking was selling something and said "*...this is your opportunity to make a difference...*"

I looked at the clock and it said eleven oh seven
I had to get this last order to Friendship Township's Elementary School by five in the morning tomorrow,
which I would even if I drove a hundred miles slower than the posted speed limit,
but I had planned on getting to the hotel tonight so I could just wake up, make the delivery and then go back to the hotel for a few hours before making the drive home to Grimace
The hotels my company book me at never had twenty-four hour check-in times
It was either check in at three pee em,
or you were shit outta luck
I loaded up the GPS and saw that I was two hours from Friendship and another thirty-five minutes from Friendship

Township Elementary School

Jan left the diner,
wrapping the sash of a thin coat around her waist as she hustled toward a car
She dropped her keys before sticking them into the lock and when she bent over to pick them up, I saw the skin of her ass, as white as winter snow
On her left cheek there was ink,
but I couldn't tell very well what had been drawn
She grabbed the keys and continued into her car
As she began to drive off,
she noticed me,
and slid to a stop next to the driver-side window

We each rolled down the glass of our vehicles
and she smirked

"Thought that was you," she said, "what ya still doin' here?"
"Just takin' a break," I said, "though I didn't mean to stay this long. I shoulda been at my hotel by now."
"Listen, thanks again for earlier."
"It's no problem really. I meant to do something more. Those assholes at the table there makin' that comment about ya. I wanted to hurt them,"
I had this image of being able to slam the face of the one guy in the hardback coat into his plate, so hard that it'd knock him out
"I'm just not really a strong guy, I guess. They'd kick my ass somethin' horrible and I'd probably have to quit my job it'd be so bad."
"Just you wanting to do something like that, is more than anyone has ever really done for me, though," she said, "so, you're still a good man for that thought."
"Yea, but wantin' to do somethin' hasn't always gotten done what *needs* done, ya know?"
"You have a name?"

"Yea, do you?"
She laughed.
"You already know my name," Jan said, "I'm askin' for yours."
"Jerry," I said
"By your tone it doesn't sound like you like your name very much."
"It's not so much the name I don't like so much as the person who gave it to me"
"Mom or dad?"
"Mom," I said,
"she used to say the name 'Jerry' is strong and resilient to a lot of things life can throw at ya. She'd say because of this name, I'd take on life's challenges *better* than a lot of people normally would. I always thought it sounded more like I'd been named after a peanut processing company. Like *Planter's*."

Jan shook her head with a chuckle
"I like it. I knew a Jerry once. Well, a Gerald."
"A Gerald is just a fancy Jerry," I muttered
"His parents were fancy. Gerald was a cunt,"
Jan left with a nod, saying she hoped to see me again
I told her I travel a lot for work, so there's always a chance

Her tailights went east
My headlights pointed west

The Ghost of Uninterrupted Pleasantries

I was alone
With everything behind
Everything ahead
The crow's beak like stone
The crow itself like air
Here was a bird that had no fear
I was a man with only a windshield
The blend of the moments all mixing together
What was there to do
when I wasn't doing any of it

What is there to do
when I don't want to do any of it
I remember a time when I was excited
Excitement for the day
I was aroused by the thought of dawn
And dusk likewise
Something has changed in me
Perhaps there is too much inside
They say too many memories can make a man
Go insane
Too many memories make a man
Divided and severred
Cut up and pulled-apart
Too many memories
Not enough purpose
The good and the enjoyable dawn gone and etched on stones
stuck in the ground
Where more satisfied people wait underground in boxes
Wait to be eaten by memories
In the dark, they have peace
Uninterrupted
Unhindered by hindrances of a mind

The road does that to you
The road adds kindling
The road has no desires or lusts or lingering dread
The road makes a man
See himself

And when a man sees himself
All that can save him are his memories

For those next three or four months,
Jerry might have gone completely insane if it weren't for Grimace
The cat waited for him every day
And during Jerry's longer stretches on the road, the nice old lady neighbor next door would feed him, although to her credit, she had to do so from a distance
Grimace didn't like anyone's company except for Jerry's
Since leaving the office job, Jerry had fallen in love with the road and all of its many unexpected facets
He would go back to January's Diner too,
Sometimes just for coffee
Other times for a full-plated breakfast
Each time he walked through those diner doors,
There she was
January
And after miles and miles of driving and hotels and hypnotic thoughts on the consistency of concrete to dirt, January became the glue that held the fractioning pieces of Jerry's mind together

All the roads led back to her
He could feel his mind being pulled apart
But there were days in which he felt them rejoining their edges into different shapes
New shapes he'd no recollection of learning about in school
And for the first time
He couldn't tell if he were sane and going crazy
Or if he'd been crazy all along,

And only now had begun to see the truth of that insanity

January suspected there must be something odd enough about him, something he wasn't willing yet to explain, but she knew that of all men
All men had a past
All women had a curiosity too, she knew
But not all women shared patience
Whenever he came into her diner,
He would eat, and leave
He never once fouled her existence with a request to see the inside of his truck,
Or accompany him to his hotel room,
He was pleasant, and that was new for her
And as long as Jerry kept coming into the diner,
January knew had something to look forward to

The hotel lights gleamed back at me
The lady at the front desk had a pair of tits weighed down by years,
but mostly gravity
Beyond that, she had a shape like a
Matryoshka doll,
those Russian wooden carved toys where you open one up and there's a smaller one inside
She had the shape of the outer-most doll
The one that felt like a fat cock when you held it in one hand

She looked like she could use a drink
She took my ID and said I had a good lookin' face, I turned my head another way to show her it was really me,
and she laughed because that was what I guess she did before blushing
When she realized I had a bag full of booze,
she turned with a different temperament in mind altogether

She said
"boy I could really use a drink"
I said
"I've got a bag full of booze"
She said
"probably not the stuff I'm into"
I told her that's an
irresponsible assumption,
“After enough drinks of this stuff, it could be something you'll never not be into”
rode the elevator to the second floor,
and threw my bags down onto the bed

Three rounds and our song is over

I stretched and my bones in my spine
broke
snap
all of them at once

my whiskey is eating away at the wax at the bottom of this
paper cup
this paper cup doesn't have a chance
I don't
Have a chance
Not against him
He's so intellectual, she says
He's into art
He has a mustache that she digs
for some fucking reason
but he's a kid, and that
makes her a pedo in my book

when I left, I had
a dream that I killed him
but I don't have that in me
I'm too soft
Killing is for other people
People with purpose
I'm just a guy in a hotel
Between jobs
Between routes
And outside it's snowing
It makes me miss her
I don't think she's mine anymore

On a trip a little further than what I was used to,
There'd been placed outside of the hotel
A statue of a man
But he was red-skinned
A native american
Red chief
He had a red face and a big nose
And over his shoulders were draped colorful blankets made by his people
In the center of his chest had been stuck a stereo speaker
The mesh was old and worn out,
It looks as though something had tried to eat its way in
The speaker turned on as I walked passed
Out of its mesh a voice tried to say something
But it just sounded static,
High-pitched
and probably something in high spirits
but I couldn't make out a word

Seeing about a girl I knew in grade school

There's an early morning whisperer telling me sweet
nothings,
they saw my chest hair last night peek out from the buttons of
my dress black shirt

Last night she said
"now there's a man's warmth"
This morning she's nowhere to be found,
and outside my hotel room door
the sound of fleeing footfalls scatter and thunder away

What a night
What a morning

She lived nearby, turns out
So close
her house was only just over the bridge
From the hotel my
Legs began to shake
It'd been twenty years, at least, since last we knew of each other's existence
We never even said hello to each other in the halls
We never shared a wall of lockers
We weren't ever on each other's radar
But there she lived
With two kids
And a piece of shit husband

We sat in the coffee shop and she looked like a woman who doesn't drink much coffee but
values her coffee whenever she has it
She said I looked like someone who had left something behind,
Something I'd yet to confront,
She said people try to hide that sort of thing,
Only a few are ever good at it
I told her she's not wrong,
There *was* a decision that did have to be made
But that day could be far off
It could be tomorrow
It could be months from now
I said the people in charge of making that decision
Niether one of them want anything to do
With making it
I said neither one of us are fans of confrontation
Whether it's confronting people
Or ideas

The coffee tasted black
Dark smooth and rich
The foam on top slowly vanished

into the darkness
She drank from a mug shaped to her hands
And she said it was good and warm,
Good for her hands
Outside the snow still clung to the ground
The air
too cold for it to melt just yet

There's something to this woman,
this girl I knew from school
Looking at her is
dreamlike
And in a perfect dream, she exists
If I woke up from that dream and she wasn't there
I know I'd be held down by more than just your average
Wednesday-night sadness

Months from now
Close to Fall
Before it's Winter again
Her divorce will be final
And her happiness restored
I'll ask her
"How's the bed?"
And she'll say
"I was able to get some screws in it a while back. Supported
with a paint bucket secretly, just in case."

Regardless of how we chose to fill our time together from
that moment on,
our conversations about sharing the bottle of red wine we'll
in all likelihood never have
Will remain a constant framed nothing hanging on the wall

Darlings of the Unexplained

You can't seem to breathe
Not because your lungs have forgotten how

It is a nameless agony,
To wait, remembering

You could kill the next person to walk through the door,
Squeeze the voice from their throat
Just to start a conversation

It all sounds like a good idea,
But you lay there doing nothing at all,
You brain feeling like it's wrapped in cellophane
Not wanting to spend the rest of your life dying

Don't be a cunt

Must you spend your waking minutes
reminding me of all the times I said mean
nasty
things to you,
What is
an apology
if it's not followed by forgiveness?
I've sacrificed
Now it's your turn
That's how it works, damnit
I apologize
You forgive
Or if it's your fault
You apologize
And I forgive
That's how it works
Have you forgotten?
You keep doing this thing
You keep expecting and assuming
I've been there
I've expected and been left short
I've assumed
And been tested positive for bacteria
I've been punched in the mouth for less
Even the waitress at the diner has the common decency to not take it to heart if my pockets are low and I have to short change her
I'll get her tomorrow, I'll say, and she'll smile
Because she forgives
Forgive me, goddamnit
Don't be a cunt

Betrayal

I'm back on alcohol and I'm better than ever
Sadness feels like spunk at the breakfast table,
Grief is my new best friend,
But only
because my old best friend tried to fuck my wife
Grief is better

How many horses have to surrender their manes to reinforce
the concrete wall of grief?
And the soldiers
bringing the word through the arteries on the way to our
hearts,
where do they stop for respite
and do the women there let them fuck them?
Are the women all virgins willing to bleed?

Threshold

In the dimness of morning unwant,
I reached back and felt that she was very much
Already wet
I grabbed her hand and led it over to my
Hard cock of dawn
It was the only thing to do,
I needed to feel her
And she was a good fuck

I soaked myself into her wetness,
Slipping into her
Hot center

When we were done,
I stretched my bones and ligaments,
And sat back so everything could amalgamate
Into
Focus

I realized I'd only written a few pages,
With so many more having been intended
More work needed to be done
Something was missing that allowed the words to flow so freely
What was once a sure thing was now a
Mass of
Calcified ejaculant,
Moving through my cock like some
Belligerent tenant refusing to leave the property

As I sat there, I could still
smell her scent on the tips of my fingers,
And so, there was still hope

III: blender/
the lover,
the novel,
the groan

Before Jerry was a liar,
He was a writer, not yet a novelist, but a writer
Some might call that being an honest liar
Because anyone who read his words would be prone to believe it was all a fiction
No one ever expected someone with as bland a face as Jerry's to write something truthful,
"Something from the heart," as writer's say
And that was the problem with his first novel

The book was to be a western, you see,
A love story,
And also a period piece taking place in the 1980's
Jerry's favorite music originated from that decade, and so the tune was to play a special part in his words
He'd had a hard time at first,
Only writing around ten pages,
That was when he was writing a western
But he scrapped the idea when he woke up one morning vomitting blood,
His conscience told him he shouldn't exploit a night of alcoholic servitude for the sake of art

The second attempt he got a little further,
Jerry wrote fifty-nine pages,
That was when the western took on a more romantic color,
But he tossed those pages out when his girlfriend at the time decided Jerry wasn't enough for her, and began seeing another man involved in a different type of art altogether: the muddy affair of pottery

When Jerry found out about them, naturally it hurt,
He couldn't bare the thought of allowing those fifty-nine pages to remain, seeing as though he gave birth to those words while the woman he loved was giving her love to someone else

The third attempt didn't come about until nearly two years later,
Jerry couldn't get his head on straight, it seemed,
He couldn't even remember why he wanted to be a writer in the first place
He would drink often, because that's what writers do, or at least writers liked to be seen as drinkers
He would go to bars alone,
Hoping to find some inspiration while engaging in an act that soon became a favorite of his: people watching,
Occasionally, he even enjoyed the company of the opposite sex in more ways than purely conversational

But as time went on, even the third attempt at writing his novel passed into the past,
He fought the urge to save it,
To revive those excellent ideas he once thought would change the way people saw love and revenge

One day,
He took an office job
He didn't know it then,

But taking that job was to be his great, although not entirely final, moment of “no turning back”

IV: Linden Worrel/ the Coalman

Sir Walter Raleigh

the queen sifted her silk
and ordered him back
they loved for a while
Longer than before
in the dark concrete chambers
in the dark spaces between sight and sense
and it was in those crevices she told him the truth
and when he heard the truth,
he left
and never returned

but the queen was a vengeful ruler
for he did return one day
and it was by her order

when Sir Walter Raleigh returned
he returned in chains

The strays were out again
Just a few of the gang of street tuffs were camped out in the back lot
At night,
their ritual orgies fill the black air with
shrieks of erogenous agony,
and ecstasy
During the day,
they ensnare baby deer from the woods and make jewelry out of their entrails for their queen
These cats will eat you in more ways than one,
and the three I crossed paths with have such mean faces,
they'll watch and listen as the others tear you to pieces

Grimace hates them,
And he loves them
The sliding door faces out into part of the back lot
He'll sit looking through the glass
He'll paw at the glass
He'll howl and whine
Sometimes they'll put on a show for him
There are at least seven or eight of the creatures
There are gray ones
A few tuxedos
A tabby or three
I've lost count
Every morning I see them scatter as I approach
Sometimes they'll have made camp in the wheel wells of my work van
Sometimes they sit and watch me from afar
I've decided they don't exactly like me
They must think Grimace is one of them
And I'm holding him hostage
He is my prisoner and perhaps one day
I will earn my comeuppance
I don't think Grimace knows this

His face can always be taken for confusion whether he's
staring out the window
Or waiting for me to feed him
I can't read Grimace like a person
But still, I feel as though we are connected
We were meant to be, he and I
When he dies,
I'll bury him out back so the strays can
dig up his corpse and
eat him
Because I know that that's
what they really want to do

Don't call the fire department, the marquee is (not) on fire

The road signs came together like moth wings
Flapping in slow motion
The bronze liquid fell into the glass
Like moth wings
Flapping
In
Slow
Motion
I hear the train at midnight
Like every other midnight
The sound of that train is a heartbeat of the dark
The night's pulse

My eardrums
are mirrors to sparkling constellation
Songs we made out to in high school
Have more meaning now,
The girls we knew in early elementary
Are now mothers of two,
Rearranging their own century
Nature doesn't need to kill us all
It only needs to kill enough of us to make
The rest of us
Go crazy
But as we sociopaths know,
It's always different when it happens to us

"If we tell them our secrets
Then our dreams will outlive us,"
she was naked as she said this,
her breasts perfect in their middle age hang
And I was heading out the door too fast, still hard
but no longer hungry

There was a coupon resting on the counter for fifty bucks off
my next tax preparation
I wasn't sure why I put it there
Or if I was the one who put it there
The whole thing just screams SETUP
Grimace wanted something and so I was up
What else could it be besides another plate of food?
I scraped off the dried up shit from the last time I fed him
and it plopped into the trash can
His ears perked up at the sound of a new can opening
And as I slammed the can down onto the plate
The food spilled over onto the porcelain
He sat by his spot
The look of fake appreciation in his eyes
I called him an ungrateful son of a bitch
Because that's what all cats are
He dove down into the food pink nose first
until his face disappeared entirely
He ate so quickly he was already digesting

The coupon for
money off my next tax preparation gleamed in an untrue
light of impending dawn shining through the sliding glass
door
I must have found it some night while at Jaunty's the bar on
the corner of Albert and Granny Smith where only the
blacks went
I wasn't black but they welcomed me anyway
They said I had the face of a white man but the balls of Fred-
erick Douglass, and the shadow of a young Mike Tyson
Whatever the hell that meant

I noticed on the coupon a number
Handwritten by someone
By the way the three was written like a fat woman with the
majority of her mass in her ass,
I'd be a liar to say it wasn't written by me

Next to the number was a name: Linden Worrel
Followed by:
"call me, would love to talk shop with ya"
Oh fuck
Grimace heard me
He was already inside his shithouse but he still heard me
His head peeked out to make sure I was okay
Oh fuck
I said again
Grimace let a turd fall out of his ass
It sounded like someone squeezing a
ketchup bottle
He then jettisoned out of his shithouse and skidded to a stop just in time to crawl under the bed in the next room
Oh fuck
I didn't give a shit about the tax preparation coupon

Linden Worrel, like me, had a few published books to his name, and not self-published, like some of these fakers soaking the streets with their own vomit, but actually published by a real publisher, and he was proud of that
He wrote contemporary fiction mainly from his "own personal experience", but one conversation with the guy and unless you were a deaf patron frequenting Hank's Whore House, you knew he was full of hot shit
Linden Worrel had been at Jaunty's because *unlike* me, he actually was black
So black, in fact, I used to call him the Coalman at parties
The parties I used to always be invited to
Parties where only writers attended and drank wine from bottles blown from glass more costly than any of our mother's funerals
Linden Worrel was also very proud of his blackness
He wore purple a lot

His favorite flower was the teasel though I'm not sure why;
it doesn't even look like a flower
Our only real area of common ground,
other than being writers,
Was that we both enjoyed Miles Davis, though him longer than me
I could say with at least half-confidence I'd only just begun to enjoy his music sometime within the last year
Linden Worrel was so black and so old, he could say he once knew the motherfucker, and I might believe him

Linden Worrel knew I didn't like him,
So why he'd given me his number was beyond me
Had I gotten so drunk that I'd forgotten what kind of a horrible writer he is?
What had we been talking about while so deftly and recklessly falling further and further under the influence?
I dialed his number
Because
I think I was still a little
drunk from the night before
Three rings and nothing
But on the fourth ring the tone *clicked*
He picked up
"Hullo," his voice was raspy, like someone who's been playin' a saxophone since he was eleven
"Coalman," I asked, my voice just as raspy, but not for the same reasons
"Jerry?"
"I have your number right here," I said
"You do? How is that?"
"You *gave* it to me," I replied
"That doesn't sound like somethin' I'd do, and it sure as shit don't sound like somethin' you'd ask for," he said
"I agree,"
"So what are ya doin' callin' me?"

“I dunno,” I said, “thought maybe you’d wanna get a drink some time,” I looked down at the tax preparation coupon, “talk shop, or...”

“...yea, yea I guess we could do that, how’s Jaunty’s tonight?”

“The same as every other night I’d imagine,” I said

“No, I mean, how ABOUT Jaunty’s tonight?”

“Yea, how bout it?”

“Just be there at dark, Jerry, sweet Jesus ya damn drunk,” he said and hung up the phone

Old Lexi ain't for everyone

Jaunty's was like a fire you see from far away
and all the blacks are drawn to it when the sun goes down
the building is made of earth
like a mountain older than the dinosaurs
there's one bouncer,
though he's so big he probably doesn't bounce very well and just goes right through the ground to the other side of the globe

Jaunty's
used to be owned by a man named Jaunty
But Jaunty's been dead for three generations of the black man's blood
Holding the keys to the kingdom now
Was a man named Clarence
Clarence King, aptly named
Some distant cousin of Jaunty, they shared very little blood
But some say
Clarence looks like Jaunty in the eyes when the moon is touched by clouds just right
I always wonder how that could be
How could anyone alive today remember what Jaunty looked like
I know it doesn't matter
And shouldn't matter
I don't deserve to know
I'm the only white man in the whole house
And for some reason, I'm welcome
They all raise their glasses when they see me
They all call me Jerry and
Pass me a smoke
They say "Jerry! How ya been?"
And I say "Good, good, like the prettiest pile of shit at the end of the alley!"
And they say, "I dunno about a pile of shit, but you sure are the prettiest puddle in the whole goddamn ocean!"
They laugh and cough on their smoke and their drinks dribble down their brown lips over their brown chins
And we sit and our asses sink into the cushions still clinging to the tops of barstools

"Clarence," one man calls out
Clarence is behind the bar
He's cleanin' glasses and slaps the rag over his shoulder like a naughty child's ass
"Wut," he calls back
"Get my man Jerry here a drop of Old Lexi,"
he says
"Old Lexi? That ain't for beginners,"
Clarence laughs
"Old Lexi is precisely for beginners,"
the man insists
"I ain't a beginner," I call out
"You're a beginner here," Clarence says
"Honestly just any old whiskey will do me right," I say
Clarence looks to me and slides me a glass of the cheapest stuff they got
I raise the glass to my nose and smell it
Old carpet, I think, with a discolored crust on top
That's what it smells like
"I'll introduce ya to Old Lexi some other time," Clarence says, "she's not an easy woman to take down..."
"Are any of them," I ask
"Yes," Clarence glows with knowledge and experience, "yes, there are some"

Jaunty's was alive
I walked to the front and the bouncer seemed happy to see me
He said "Jerry, I didn't think to see ya again so soon. Two nights in a row, same white man, that's almost like putting a curse on a house, don't ya think?"
I told him I didn't know much about curses
Maybe Clarence might have a better response
I told him I was invited by Linden Worrel
"He was here last night too," the bouncer said
"Yea, apparently we talked enough to warrant further conversation," I said
"Well, he's not here, but you can head on inside, it's kind of a slow night in there, Clarence will be happy for the business," he said
I went inside
Most of the stools were empty
Only three guys in the whole place,
Including Clarence behind the bar
A rag was slung over his shoulder and he was leaning forward in front of a patron
Their mouths moved as if in conversation
But the TV was so loud I couldn't hear the words
Clarence looked up when he saw someone had walked in
When he saw it was me, he
Laughed, slamming the bar top with the palm of his left hand and the whole of his forearm
"Old Lexi isn't in tonight,"
he said loudly over the TV
I told him I wasn't here for her
I said to give me the same stuff I had last night
The stuff that smelled like old carpet
Clarence slid me a glass
and I waited for Linden Worrel

Linden Worrel arrived no later than my third drink

And by then I was already feeling like I could eat anything in the world and shit gold
I remembered him being shorter,
But that may have been due in part to me never liking him very much
I never did have any masculine respect for the guy
I never enjoyed his writing,
I never could understand why anyone at all could enjoy his writing
He even walked like a man who's never had a limp, literal or otherwise,
He opened doors with a hand so loosely clasped over the knob, he was far too appreciating of his own existence

I hated him, you could say
And,
Here
I
Was,
Hating him the same as any other day

"You live at home, alone," he said
The conversation had been going on for an hour
We were so soaked in whiskey
Regret, but also a little hope, dripped from our chins
"I have a cat," I said
"He's only a cat," he said, "a cat ain't no woman"
"Don't you ever say that again,"
I stood up, letting my glass slide to the floor
Where it crashed into a thousand shards
"He's not ONLY a cat. He makes life easier. He's a steel trap, doesn't give shit up. Which makes him more respectable than any living creature on the face of the earth. Do you know what depression is? I doubt someone as clean as you has any idea. It's when there's somethin' inside of ya that makes ya happy, maybe it fuels ya, but some days it feels

like it's not there. Maybe someone took it out of ya, stole it, took it for themselves, or, hell for fuck's sake, maybe it never existed at all. Having a cat fills that gap. He makes it all better. No woman, no matter what her pussy smells like can do that."

Linden Worrel was not an animal person
He loved women more than a lumerjack loved chainsaws
Although in one of the bios in the back of his second novel
How I Slew the Lawyer
he said he lived at home with his then wife
And a box turtle named Nefertiti
He also once said in an interview his most regretable allergy
was to that of cat dander
But I always thought it was his way of avoiding the truth
that he actually hated cats

From there, unsurprisingly,
the conversation turned to women
And he asked about my wife
He hadn't heard, of course
My private life had never been very public
And normally I wouldn't have said a word about it
Normally I wouldn't even be here
But I told him what I knew
And what I knew was that I'd done wrong
Somewhere down the line
And eventually,
she had had enough
"Listen, Jerry, I ain't one to judge one's take on any individual woman. I've had my share of brown plum pies. But she was a bitch, Jerry. A real, first class, straight up cunt. I say that to you as a friend, a fellow traveller of the female wasteland. I remember that Annual you took her too. She hung on your arm but she had eyes like daggers meant for the back. I know it hurts, a woman will do that. But the bandage is time, and nothin' else. I promise ya that."

"I don't want a bandage, I want a gun"
"Then get a gun, already. Dying is the least expensive way to heal a broken ticker, and the most permanent"
He made a gesture with his hand in the shape of a gun and held it to his own head
"I thought you wanted to come here to talk shop," I drank
Linden Worrel laughed
"Talk shop? About what? Writing? Who talks about writing? What self-respectin' writer *talks* about writing? Let me tell you something, we ARE talkin' shop right now. We're talking about life. And if you're a writer and you're talking about writing, then you're just wasting time, pure and simple, but if you're a writer and you're talking about life, then aren't you talking about writing too? Life is all about time-management, Jerry. The same things happens to everyone at one time or another. The *same* damn things. How can you sit there with that drink and pretend to know how to manage that time if you're *talking* about writing?"

But I wasn't a pretender
I wasn't claiming to know anything
Much less how to manage my time
But he was right about one thing
Maybe I shouldn't ever talk about writing again
Maybe I should just write something
Sure
I could go home
Say hello to Grimace
Open a new bottle or finish the old one or both
And just write
I could write the next greatest novel ever written
I could write a poem and talk about "edge"
And how life has fucked me more than the average woman
Crap
There I go talking about writing again

Stray cat come home

I lay down on my back
Taunting the gods
Watching the storm from
down below
on the hard grassy dirt
beneath the plane's white smoke streek across the sky
am I not doing enough
am I not doing my part

history will wake up from its nap soon
and when it does
it
will
be
hungry

Unstoppable

They all had a fair chance at taking my heart,
But there was a catch too
Every woman I met was a glimpse at my next downfall
My next plummet
My next rock bottom
The next hole I'd find myself sinking deeper into

Every smile was a future chest pain
Every laugh an aching kidney
I loved and I hated them
They all could take me down
And they all would eventually
Chipping away at me
And if the drink doesn't kill me
Enough of them will have chipped away at my crust
Until one final bitch emerges from the slime
A woman will eat you whole one night
A single mouthful
She will shit you out the next morning
And forget your name by noon
They
Are
Unstoppable

V: ReBirth from the Great Big Pussy/ she knew what she was doing from the start

Double LP

the death came as the door closed
I'd drank as much as they said it would take
And now they were no longer just
annoying assholes with something to say
They were all
Psychics
With signs that now had merit
Now everyone would come to them for answers
They will say
"you knew when that drunk would die"
"you knew when he'd take his last breath"
"you knew"

As the story goes for everyone
Someone always knows
when it's going to happen,
Just not us

Linden Worrel had given me the drugs and
They tasted a little like concrete mixture and
The skin of a monstera leaf
He'd said,
"Like any drug you've never taken, take it at home, and try to have a plan, try to give yourself something to do that isn't unsafe, and if all possible, have a sober chaperone."

I took the drugs at home
Before starting to chew, I told myself to throw a load of my darks in the wash, and to use very little detergent
I told myself to order a pizza and to have the delivery driver bring it inside for an extra few bucks tip
I did not have a chaperone
Grimace didn't count
Grimace wasn't dependable that way
He saw me sit down on the couch and crawled into my lap
But he offered no words of supportive assurance that he'd make the call to the proper medical persons if the situation plummeted into realms of unrecoverable sanity

I sunk into the couch like a bag of trash forgotten about and left on the curb, and Grimace was with me
Purring
Sixty-five minus forty-two minutes later and
I threw him across the room
The chainsaw exploded against the far wall into a hundred pieces, the chain embedding into the drywall
I heard a meow,
But I think that might have just been my stomach
My stomach did that sort of thing from time to time
And it was Sunday so of course my stomach was meowing
"It's not working, Grim," I said

I decide it was time I should start my laundry
But before that a more pressing matter rose to the surface:

The wall needed to be patched up,
I knew this because last week, Grimace's friend
The Hundred-Mile Smile, a snow fox with a fat ass, that Grimace refused to kill and eat and instead befriend, had headbutted the wall, causing a contusion that led to the landlady having to phone a house-calling doctor just to get an assessment

The doctor said I should be the one responsible for patching the hole because one
Snowfoxes aren't real
And Two
The indentation looked more like someone with an angry fist had lost control of his emotions

I agreed to patch the hole only because I didn't have any other place to live

But the strange thing now was
The hole was gone
I couldn't find it
There was nothing there
Just a smooth wall
That and a chainsaw chain embedded in the material
I touched the chain
And heard a meow
Was my stomach meowing again?
I touched the chain once more
And the meow returned
Weird

I walked through the swamp the same as I had before,
Just the shallow end first, the flesh-eating gnats usually stuck to the deep parts, and that's not where I was headed yet
No need for getting completely filthy either just yet
I lifted up the corpses

Turning over their heads and even looking into their mouths
I used a forefinger and my thumb to remove a tooth from the lower mandible of one mouth, there was light shining from beneath it
But when I peered into the socket
All I saw was starlight
It was too bright to see anything else
I put the tooth back
It slid right back into the socket
And *clicked* like a light switch
Returning to the dim,
I continued my search

A week went by
And nothing
A Year
And I only felt older
The wallpaper had begun to peel in places I thought I'd fixed with glue
Every now and then a bug would crawl out and then crawl back in
Little bumps swarmed beneath the wallpaper in every room of the apartment
They swarmed like armies, some of them poking through
Their little black bug heads with their nine silver eyes
All of them crawling and watching

Another year went by and suddenly they were gone
The wallpaper had peeled all the way back and now the walls were just bare
Wooden slats rotten around the edges
I convinced myself to not care about the wallpaper
But to rather go outside for a while
Get some fresh air
It had in fact been over a year since I'd walked outside and felt the sun

My skin would be grateful, if anything
I packed a backpack
Because I planned on staying outside for at least a few days

Into the bag
I stuffed a loaf of bread
But I forgot the butter(I wouldn't remember this until sometime during the following week and by then it wouldn't matter anyway, because you know what they say about butter)
I threw in a necklace my mother used to wear at Sunday dinners
She was buried with it,
Or so everyone thought
What they didn't know is that before they locked her up in that ten-thousand dollar box,
I snuck in and ripped it from her neck
After the necklace, I felt the weight, and felt there needed to at least be a few bottles of water thrown in
I might get thirsty

I opened the front door,
The backpack slung over my back
And it was then I noticed something different about the outside
For one,
It was dark
And there was a stench
Not a bad smell,
But hot and wet

And there seemed to be a groan emitting from
Somewhere
Up ahead
A groan
Or was it a moan?
There's a difference between a moan and a groan?
Yes there is, shut the fuck up, this is my roadshow

There seemed to be an indiscernable amount of pleasure
Within that moan
She wanted more
She wanted it to keep going

And suddenly,
From the depths of the nothingness that lay ahead,
The unmistakable shape of a giant cock surged toward me,
It surged forward once,
Twice,
Three times
And each time there was that same moan
The thick, girthy bastard was thrust in,
And I was forced to duck away or be crushed by the cock
I dove forward into the geranium bushes I'd planted with my own two hands into the garden,
I screamed as the cock returned
And from the darkness the moaning continued
Once more the cock emerged, and
From the tip
A small hole opened like a tired eyelid
And from that opening exploded a geyser of white fluid
The fluid rained down all around me
Filling in the cracks in the earth
Forming puddles near where the road met the curb
And the stuff kept on coming
There was no end
The cock spit and spat

"You're goin' to die one day just like everyone else"

The voice was my father's

"And when that day comes, the light will leave your eyes and there won't be anything left after"

The cock spit and spit and it wasn't long before I was forced to swim
The white stuff
Whatever it was
Formed a lake
I swam for as long as I could
But my arms were tired
And the stuff was heavy
A different consistency than the water found in regular lakes
This stuff was thick and milky, more thick than milky
And it smelled faintly sweet

The cock was gone, finally,
and the moaning had ended
But I was still swimming
Every now and then I felt something tug at my feet
Or what I thought was something tugging at my feet
How could there be anything down there
I was the only one here

Below the surface
See anything
I could
Not

There was just me
Swimming in the dark as best as I could

And then
Then it all went sideways
The dark grew darker
And I tasted something new

Jerry realized very quickly that he had not heard my voice since page 100,
The angelic, somewhat femanine voice that was sometimes capable of conveying comfort
But for him generally reminded him of the pain of the past
and for some reason he remembered very clearly that the last words I had spoken were "no turning back"

This realization manifested as the darkness finally took him
And the Lake of Semen finally rose to levels too high and the tide barked too madly for him to hang on any longer
His strength left him
As it would have left any man in his position
But he had lasted longer than he'd assumed he'd be able to
and
Jerry was comforted by the idea that for all his faults,
For everyone he'd ever inflicted pain towards
He might
He just might be able to outswim any man to have ever lived

But that feat of strength was not enough to save him
Jerry knew in his heart that he had done all he could
It was up to fate if he was to survive

Maybe if he did survive,
he'd look back on this day and write about it
No one would read it though,
And anyone who did would become helplessly
lost in an abyss of muddied and bitter confusion
He sank into the Lake of Semen
Sinking lower and lower
He tasted the fluid as it entered his mouth
It was sweet in a rude, unwelcome sort of way
And he thought maybe there might be a positive
end to this madness
Until the semen began to fill his lungs
And as all dreams do before they stop being
dreams,
all went to black

It's time I admitted it all finally
I killed my wife
I had to
The strain of pretending became too much
When I'd found out what she'd done
I tried to tell myself this was what all adults go through
Marriage isn't perfect
Not for anyone
It may have moments of perfection sprinkled throughout
But never has there ever been a marriage that had more perfection
Than
Horror
I got away with it too
They thought it was a suicide
No one questioned anything because they all knew she was depressed

Actually
I didn't kill her
I didn't pull the trigger
The more accurate way to put it
Is that I knew she was dying on the inside
And when she finally did what she said she was going to do for all those years,
I didn't do anything to stop it from happening

Telephone operator: *sir, are you still there? Sir?*

Jerry: *have you had your bananas?*

Telephone operator: *I'm sorry, excuse me?*

Jerry: *they're supposed to help against the hangover*

Telephone operator: *I'm not drinking, wait, what does this have to do with?*

Jerry: *the drugs, though, I'm not sure anything can help against those*

Telephone operator: *are you sure you're alright, sir?*

Jerry: *My life is in stunning 4k, my soul has just let me know I'll be okay, I can see every drop of blood, and none of it's green or blue, I'll be fine*

Telephone operator: *Sir, I'm going to send an officer and an ambulance to your residence, just to be sure. You might think you're okay, and maybe you are, but this is just standard procedure. I hope you understand. If you don't mind, I'd like you to please stay on the line*

Jerry: *I'll stay for a little while*

Telephone operator: *They'll be there in approximately nine minutes*

Jerry:

Telephone operator: *sir?*

Jerry:

Telephone operator: *sir, are you still there?*

Jerry:

The grass I lay on was wet with morning dew
Somewhere a sprinkler was *ch-ch-ch-ch-ch*-ing
I can't be sure when the drugs wore off
But when they did,
It felt like years had passed
Having stretched onward
Like someone's sick joke
waiting for the punch line to sink in
Half my left hand had dug itself into some mud
My fingernails were filled,
caked with cold soil
There lingered
the faint taste of chlorine on the roof of my mouth
And I thought for a hard three minutes
I was nineteen years old again

I'll never take those drugs again
I should stick to drinking
Drinking never did this to me
No matter how bad it got
The morning after was at least sympathetic
But this
This was mockery
Fuck that Linden Worrel and his drugs
Fuck that son of a bitch

Anger

she was still a bitch
And I was still a moron

How is it that the truth of our world has
Come to this
I feel crazy for staying
I'd feel worse if I left
These slabs of colorful stone
Lining our shelves
Don't do anything
Stones can't give peace
They're rocks
They're minerals
They're crystals
They're pretty to look at
But so are most women
They don't actually have any spiritual value
Our spirits will dissipate with or without them
And the bodies we leave behind
Will sink into the mud

Revenge of the Cat

there was shit everywhere
And in the middle of it all
Sat Grimace
He saw that I was home
He didn't give half of one of his shits
I should take a lesson from the cat

High at my Mother's Funeral

She'll die eventually,
I remember thinking

She'll die and it'll all be over for her
All her pain
All her agony
All her dementia
All her memories she never knew she had
Will I be the same *me* when she dies
Will she remember who I am before the end

Probably not
In all likelihood,
I should just consider her dead now
The racist bitch
Boy
She really turned into some kinda monster
I don't even recognize her anymore

Back again

Figured I should explain something while I can
the process, that is
I've met many women along the way who say I should at least talk about my feelings
They say a man's emotions turn them on,
And when the truth is about them,
The lips between their legs really start to flap
Like yard flags on the fourth of july
They'll ask you to strangle them,
The christians too
And they'll say it feels good,
Until you squeeze too hard and they
Remember they have lungs that need air
Their eyes bulge a little
And you can feel their body tense up as the life inside makes one last attempt to hold on
But you keep going
Because
You want to see what happens
A moment ago,
She was telling you she loved you
and you believed her,
because
sociopaths
do actually tell the truth sometimes
they do
I promise
Talk to one sometime
They open up about everything if you touch their thigh in just the right manner
Explain how the leather jacket you wear is your dead father's and they might even marry you
You might even be able to handle them
But most times, you'll need to consider the inevitable
And then there's getting rid of the body
A body doesn't move itself
And oftentimes there are obstacles
Like other people

And other people are the real problem whether you're moving a dead body or not

Years ago, when Jerry's mother died, Jerry dressed in the same tuxedo he wore to prom
It was a navy blue piece with a white shirt underneath and a blue tie slightly darker than the slacks and jacket

Jerry was not as sad as he thought he might be, even though he thought he'd be surprised by how sad he might be, he really wasn't

When his father died, he remembered crying
When his dog died, he downright balled his eyes out
But his mother's death was not the case
In fact, during the funeral reception, Jerry went to the bathroom to empty his bowels and after he stood up to wipe himself clean, he didn't even flush
He looked in the mirror while washing his hands and felt a great wave of relief
She was finally dead, he thought to himself
Dead and no more than a memory
And memories, for people like Jerry, were easy to erase

There weren't many people in attendance either,
A fact that did not surprise Jerry one bit
His mother had waned her circle of friends during her twilight years, and never once considered the notion that by the time of her death, it might become a circus act just to fill the viewing room for her casket

When it came time to speak a few words about the recently deceased, a few people did wander up to the pulpit

Eventually, all eyes turned to Jerry, expecting him to say at least something of gratitude
But he stood with his hands in his navy blue pockets and chewed a piece of neon green spearmint gum because he thought his breath smelled like onions and clove from the bagel he ate for breakfast

He didn't say anything, and they say that the great sigh of disappointment exhaled from the people can still be heard in the dreams of those who remember it

The funeral ended with her body in the ground
And Jerry thought that was a sign of a successful day

The Backyard

The remains were there
Of course
I didn't put them there
but I did provide the shovel

VI: The Long Way to Nowhere/ the road has no beginning, nor an end

Dart

thrown from the ragged hand
It lands hard with a thud
There are no cheers
There is no renown
For a dart

Linden Worrel came in through the door
he didn't say a word to me
didn't acknowledge my existence
that was to be our relationship for the duration of our future
He drank and I drank
We didn't speak of it
The act
And when he was done drinking
He left
He didn't even hold the door for the man coming in

Finally I left
The man on the corner had tears in his eyes
But they were red
I thought they must be blood
I thought that couldn't be,
Men can't cry blood
Only statues cry blood
But he spout out his tune
He said
"Now and forever, the sky tastes as it should"
And he spat at my feet
He said
"You walk amongst the godly, bow down and confess your sins"
I said I had no sins to confess
I said I was an honest man on an honest mission
To get home

I went home to my empty apartment
The cat had gone
I couldn't remember his name
I only remembered one day last week I came home
And he was gone
No note
No message

No nothing
Just
Gone
I looked out the nearest window
The one he used to look out
I saw a red bird
A cardinal, I think
It was red amongst the green brush
A flash of lightning startled the bird
And suddenly I knew its fear
The lights went out
And I heard her voice
Not my mother
Not any of the women I'd shared a bed with
Not any of the women I'd wrapped my heart strings around
The heavy boots out in the hall
she was there
She knocked politely, despite the cloud that followed
She said
"I'm here, just as you asked"

I woke up from the dream
And only for a moment did I think it wasn't a dream
But a dream it was
My records were strewn about the floor
The bottle wasn't broken though it was
Empty
There was a ringing
An echo
A wind gust rushing through the closed window
And suddenly I knew I wasn't dying
But I'd jumped ahead in line by a significant amount
And everyone behind me weren't one bit empathetic
They laughed amongst themselves
They whispered tones of
Tones
In that morning-dim room, it was not the worst of times

But it was times
And that alone was noteworthy

A Song for Wooden Cocks and Concrete Cunts

I wrote this years ago it seems
I started it the first time I took a seat on Santa's lap
The left leg
He had a strong thigh muscle, I remember
Not even a baby with a rubber ass could
fathom so much as a single bounce
I was no different
and I was sore from the moment we walked into the mall
dad said "SHUT UP AND GET IN THE CAR"
Mom said "DON'T TALK TO OUR SON THAT WAY"
Dad took her by her hair and told her to "remember last week"
I remember not knowing what that meant
But I was a child then
I grew up
I married too
I eventually knew the tribulations of a mouthy wife

Eventually you have to get another glass
You have to remember that not everyone is meant for this life
They have their own sins to sin
You're no different
Except in height
Maybe weight
But the soul of a man who wants
And the spirit a woman who doesn't want to be wanted
Are like cat shit and litter
they stick to each other
There is no language to explain it
No child to imagine a story
The bitch is carving a pumpkin on Christmas day
The alter boy is brushing his teeth
And the cat who shat
is flipping a coin

from here,
THE STARS

From here,
The stars were as they said they would be
And the earth was as blue as they promised
The glass in the porthole, though
The air through my lungs
The sound of the hum
The shuttle was not where it should be, but nothing could change that anymore

"*Windcage, this is Houston, Windcage, this is Houston, are you still there? Sir?? Confirm the date and time.*"

"Houston," I said, "this is the U.S.S. Windcage, it is January the second, zero nine thirty-seven hundred hours, we are still afloat."

"Windcage, we are going to run a few more simulations, just bare with us a little while longer."

"Houston, this is the Windcage. That's a negative on those simulations. Earth is lookin' farther away by the second. Save those simulations. We're going to enjoy the view from here."

The radio was silent for a moment, as I knew it would be when I told them my plans, but really, there was nothing more to be done

"Windcage, if you just give us a few more minutes we can give you the specifications to-"

I held on to the handle by the porthole and the rest of me continued to float
Below, the blue waters of the earth were unlike any shade of blue I'd ever seen. Nothing in the books we studied even came close to depicting just how blue they really were

"Windcage, are you reading us? This is Houston. Windcage-"
"Houston, this in the Windcage, turning off the radio now to conserve the last of our power. Goodbye and God bless you all. Windcage, out."

I turned off the radio
I looked to Worrel and he gave me a knowing look

He floated just a few meters away, having taken one last look at the control board
"It's time, Jerry," he said
"No," I said at last, "I don't think it is. Not just yet."
"I've done the math. The oxygen systems will shut off at exactly ten sixty-three hundred hours, Jerry," Worrel said, "We can still put ourselves under as long as the required systems remain functional. Do you really want to suffocate to death up here?"

I thought about it
I really put some thinking into it all
But dying in my sleep just seemed like too uneventful a way to experience the end
I looked back out the porthole at the earth
"You go ahead," I said to Worrel, "I'm just going to stay here."
"It's okay," he said, "there was very little likelihood we'd find anything up here. We all knew it was a longshot. All things considered, it was still worth it. Coming up here."
Out of sight,
moonlight was shining through someone's window
But up here, it was just another rock
Another floating piece of nothing, and everything

When I didn't respond to Worrel, he nodded and before slipping into his sleep pod, he made sure to grab from the display shelf the gold-framed picture of Apollo, his pet cat from back home
When he was snug inside, holding the framed picture, the lid closed and the sleep process began

I didn't watch him go under
Instead, I just looked outside at the earth and the stars
And waited

"I'm convinced that before the year 2000 is over, the first child will have been born on the moon."
— Wernher Von Braun, January 7th, 1972

"For me, it is far better to grasp the Universe as it really is than to persist in delusion, however satisfying and reassuring."
*– **Carl Sagan***

Dave Matthes was born and raised in Swedesboro, New Jersey. He has attended various colleges for computer engineering, automotive science and criminal justice-like degrees, though he is mostly self-educated in the subjects of World History, Philosophy, Political Science and Spirituality. During the day, he works as a service technician and system installer for the restaurant industry.

He is a writer of prose and story-driven poetry and is the author of autobiographical books "The Slut Always Rides Shotgun", its sequel "The Passive Aggressors", his post-apocalyptic western series: The Two Revolvers Saga, and The Mire Man Trilogy.

Dave presently lives in Brookhaven, Pennsylvania with his wife Sarah and their cat Hank.

To keep up to date with the current and future writings of Dave Matthes, and other nooks and crannies of his sliver of life, find him online at:

www.DaveMatthes.org
www.TheTwoRevolvers.com
www.Goodreads.com
SnapChat: boozie_smoocher
Instagram: Matthes_words